A Little Princess Story

I Didn't Do It!

Tony Ross

Andersen Press

"Princess!" shouted the Queen, pointing to the muddy floor.
"Look what you did!"

"I didn't do it!" said the Little Princess.
"Daddy, Mummy said I left mud on the floor, and I didn't."

"If Her Majesty said you did, then you must have," said the King.
"I didn't do it!" said the Little Princess.

"POO!" sniffed the Little Princess as she stomped
off into the kitchen.

"Did you eat all of my chocolate cake?" asked the Cook.
"NO!" said the Little Princess. "I didn't do it!"
and she ran out into the garden.

"Did you walk all over my radishes?" grumbled the Gardener.
"NO!" said the Little Princess. "I didn't do it!"
"Huh!" said the Gardener.

She found the Prime Minister looking at his tricycle
and scratching his head.
"Did you take my bell?" he asked.

"NO!" shouted the Little Princess, running towards the castle.
"I didn't do it!"

"Look at my horse," said the General. "Did you stick a bell on his ear?"
"I didn't do it!" said the Little Princess.

"Did you sink all my ships?" roared the Admiral.
"NOOOOO!" wailed the Little Princess. "I didn't do it!"

"And did you walk all over my nice clean washing?" asked the Maid.

"I didn't do it. I DIDN'T DO IT!" sobbed the Little Princess, and she ran away to find a friend.

"What's up?" asked the Little Prince.

"Everybody blames me for everything," sniffed the Little Princess.
She told the Little Prince all about her dreadful day.

Then the two of them climbed their Sulky Tree.

The Little Princess sat on a branch and sulked.
The Little Prince put his arm around her.

"I SAID I didn't do ANY of those things," she wailed.
"But NOBODY believes me."

"I believe you!" said the Little Prince.

The Little Princess smiled her big smile.

"Why do you believe me, when nobody else does?" she said.

"Because I did all of those things!" the Little Prince said.
"IT WAS ME . . .

. . . and I saved a bit of chocolate cake for you!"

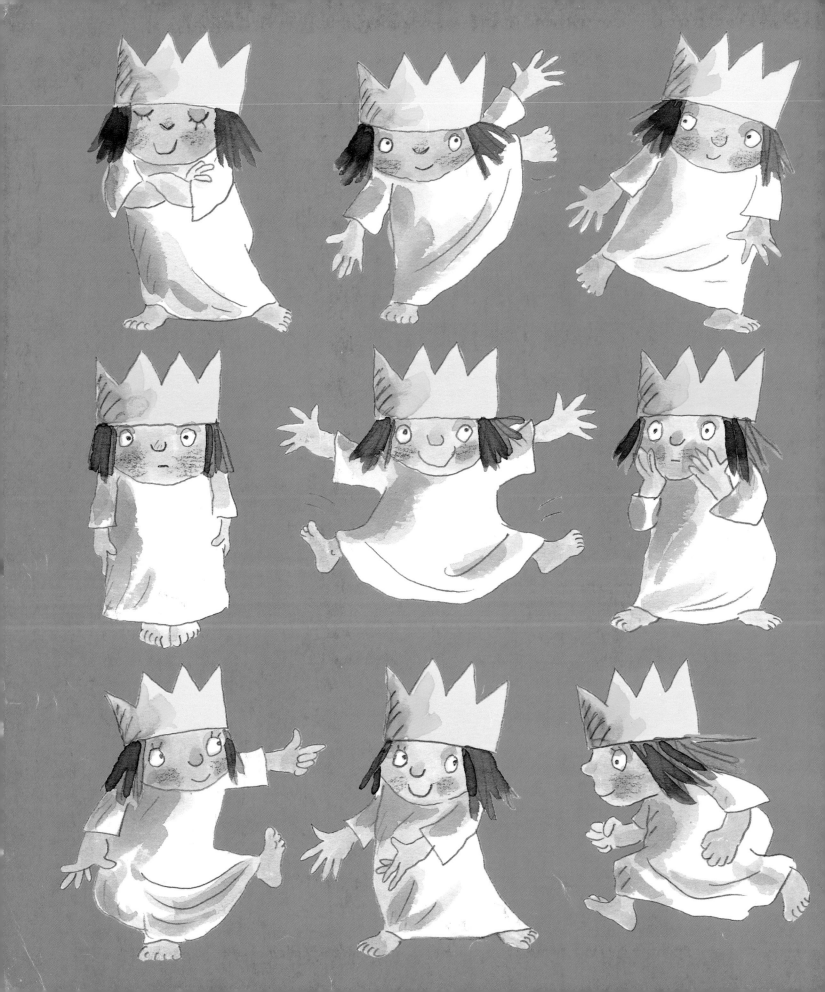